♡

To our families and K.J.S.
—A.B. & A.L.

♡

To E.P.
—J.K.

The illustrations in this book were created using watercolor textures, graphite, and Photoshop.

A portion of Abrams's profits from the sale of this book will be donated to the Child Mind Institute. For more information, visit Abramsbooks.com/product/case-of-the-zaps_9781419756726.

Cataloging-in-Publication Data has been applied for and may be obtained from the Library of Congress.

ISBN 978-1-4197-5672-6

Text © 2022 Alex Boniello and April Lavalle
Illustrations © 2022 James Kwan
Book design by Jade Rector

Printed and bound in China
10 9 8 7 6 5 4 3 2 1

Abrams Books for Young Readers are available at special discounts when purchased in quantity for premiums and promotions as well as fundraising or educational use. Special editions can also be created to specification. For details, contact specialsales@abramsbooks.com or the address below.

Abrams® is a registered trademark of Harry N. Abrams, Inc.

ABRAMS The Art of Books
195 Broadway, New York, NY 10007
abramsbooks.com

A CASE OF THE ZAPS

BY **ALEX BONIELLO** AND **APRIL LAVALLE**   ILLUSTRATED BY **JAMES KWAN**

ABRAMS BOOKS FOR YOUNG READERS • NEW YORK

Sometime in the future,
in a galaxy (not so) far away,
is a planet called

ROBOT-EARTH.

It's like Earth,
but robot-y!

And on that Robot-Earth lived—you guessed it—a robot!

Their name was 3.141592653589793238462643383279502884

Or Pi, for short.

Pi was just like most young robots.

They enjoyed playing music . . .

walking their dog . . .

hanging out with their Parental Units and friends . . .

and snacking on their favorite treat, DW-40.

As you can see, Pi had a lot on their plate.

And not just the DW-40.

One day, Pi was in school when their teacher surprised the class with an announcement.

Pack your bags, class. Next month, we'll be taking a field trip to the place that started it all:

OLDE SILICON VALLEY!

The class SPARKED with excitement.

Pi felt their circuit board BUZZ with anticipation!

Pi had always dreamed about visiting Olde Silicon Valley.

Pi spent the whole day thinking about the trip—

not only the fun times ahead, but

also all the things that could go wrong.

Later that day, Pi was walking home with their friends when—

"Are you okay, Pi?" asked RAM.

"I'm not sure . . ." Pi said.

ZAP! ZAP!! ZAP!!!

Pi's defense mechanisms JOLTED on.

"I have to go!" Pi shouted as they hurried away, feeling their cooling fans kick into OVERDRIVE.

Feeling ZAPS all around.

Feeling afraid for reasons they didn't quite understand.

WARNING!

That night, Pi tried to fall asleep,

RNING!

but they had more on their mind than usual.

WARNING!

Over the next few days, Pi tried their
best to appear calm, cool, and collected.

They tried not to think about the trip, because every
time they did, they worried that the Zaps would return.

But it seemed that the more Pi tried
to ignore the Zaps, the more space
the Zaps took up in their hard drive.

One night when Pi and their Parental Units sat down for dinner, Pi could hardly touch their DW-40. Their battery was feeling DANGEROUSLY LOW from their Central Processing Unit working overtime, when . . .

"No, no—not again," Pi said.

ZAP!

DEFENSE MECHANISMS ON!!!

ZAP!

ZAP!

Pi bolted up to their room as fast as they could, hoping to outrun the Zaps.

Mother-Board and Father-Board followed their robo-kid upstairs.

Pi usually told their Parental Units everything . . .

. . . but this was difficult to talk about.

"Something feels wrong," Pi explained. "The gears in my head are WHIRRING, and my cooling fans are going into OVERDRIVE. My danger sensors feel like they're turned up to eleven!

I'm scared I might be . . . broken."

It took all of Pi's courage, but saying

the words made them feel a little bit better.

"Pi, you're not broken! You're talking about the Zaps," Father-Board said. "I had them big-time when I was starting my new job at Space X 2. And your cousin Cosine Tangent has had them for years."

"Really?! Cosine Tangent just won the Robobell Prize for discovering a vaccine for malware!" said Pi.

"Yes, they did," said Mother-Board. "There's absolutely nothing wrong with having a case of the Zaps now and again. What's important is taking care of yourself and managing the Zaps. Let's pay a visit to Dr. Bleep Bloop in the morning."

The next day, they booted up bright and early
and rolled over to Dr. Bleep Bloop's office.

"I'm so glad you came in, and I'm proud of you for being brave and
talking to your Parental Units about all this! I know it can really get
your sprigets in a sprocket to talk about the Zaps," the doctor said.

"But why are they happening to me?" Pi asked. "What did I do wrong? I have a FIREWALL installed!"

Dr. Bleep Bloop chuckled. "Oh no, this isn't a computer virus. The Zaps can happen to anyone. Big or small, Windows or Mac, old or fresh off the assembly line."

"Anyone? But they're so scary!"

Dr. Bleep Bloop nodded. "They can feel that way. The Zaps activate your FIGHT-OR-FLIGHT sensors, even when there's no danger present."

"Oh! That explains why they make me feel like running away! So . . . give it to me straight, Dr. Bleep Bloop: Is there any cure for the Zaps?" Pi bravely asked.

"There isn't a simple cure. Part of getting over the Zaps means getting used to having them sometimes. It can be a signal that it's time to be brave. There are ways to manage the Zaps, and we can work together to make sure that your coping mechanisms have the most recent software updates."

Over the next few weeks, Pi and Dr. Bleep Bloop explored strategies to help Pi work through the Zaps.

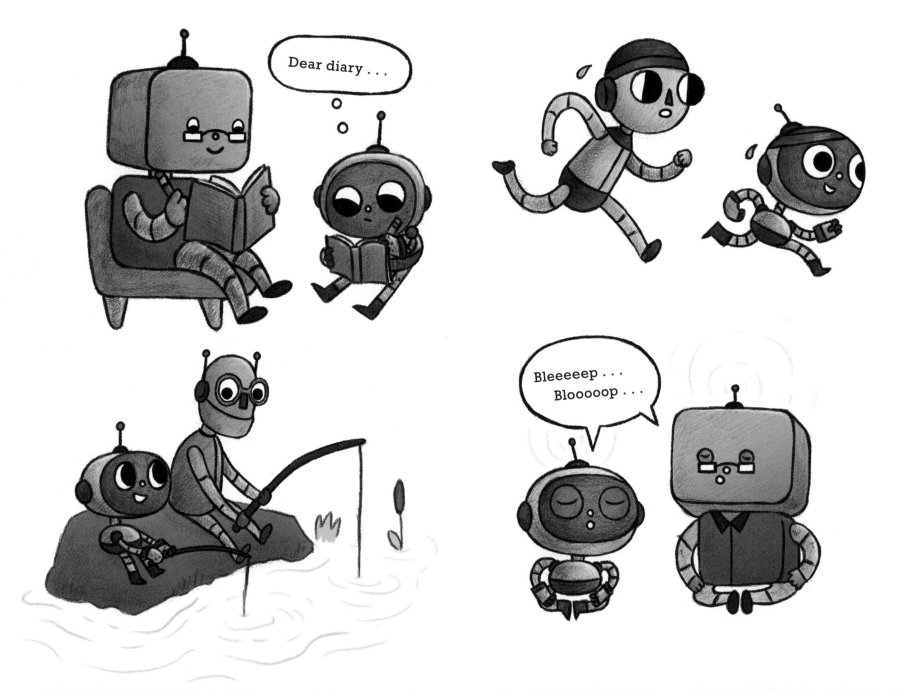

Pi even built up the courage to talk to their friends about it—and learned that one of their friends had the Zaps too!

Finally, the day of the trip to Olde Silicon Valley arrived. Armed with new skills and coping mechanisms from Dr. Bleep Bloop, Pi hopped on the bus, ready to have a great time with their class.

And Pi never had a case of the Zaps again.

JUST KIDDING! Pi had a great time on the trip, but there were certainly moments where the Zaps started to creep back in.

When that happened, Pi used the tools that Dr. Bleep Bloop had shared with them, and then the Zaps didn't feel quite so scary. It wasn't perfect, but it was a start. Pi knew that managing the Zaps would be a longtime process . . .

And robots definitely know a thing or two about processing!

A NOTE FROM THE AUTHORS

We grew up leading lives that seemed quite a bit different from each other. While April was taking dance classes, Alex was learning to skateboard. While Alex was in guitar lessons, April was becoming a very strong swimmer! Yet something we both shared, before even knowing the other, was anxiety.

It can be difficult to deal with anxiety at any point in your life, but those first experiences with it are some of the scariest. Like Pi, we both found that it was difficult to explain what we were going through, mainly because we didn't yet have the words to do so!

We hope that following Pi's journey helps you to start the conversation around anxiety with your friends and family. It can be a difficult thing to do, but once you open up, you might surprise yourself with how brave you can be. Just like Pi.

Thank you for joining Pi on their journey to understand their case of the Zaps! Whether this is your first time learning about the Zaps or you're an old pro, here are some of Dr. Bleep Bloop's favorite resources to keep the conversation going.

CHILD MIND INSTITUTE

The Child Mind Institute is an independent, national nonprofit dedicated to transforming the lives of children and families struggling with mental health and learning disorders. Its teams work every day to deliver the highest standards of care, to advance research on the developing brain, and to empower parents, professionals, and policymakers to support children when and where they need it most. Head to **ChildMind.org** for more information.

ANXIETY & DEPRESSION ASSOCIATION OF AMERICA

The Anxiety & Depression Association of America focuses on improving quality of life for those with anxiety, depression, OCD, PTSD, and co-occurring disorders through education and research. ADAA helps people find treatment, resources, and support. Visit **ADAA.org** for more information.

ASSOCIATION FOR BEHAVIORAL AND COGNITIVE THERAPIES

The Association for Behavioral and Cognitive Therapies is committed to improving health and well-being by advancing the scientific understanding, assessment, prevention, and treatment of human problems through the application of behavioral, cognitive, and biological evidence-based principles. Head to **ABCT.org** for more information.

RESOURCES!